HICKORY, DICKORY, DOCK

ROBIN MULLER ; SUZANNE DURANCEAU

HICKORY, DICKORY, DOCK

SCHOLASTIC
HARDCOVER

Scholastic Inc.

New York

Library of Congress Cataloging-in-Publication Data

Muller, Robin.
Hickory, dickory, dock / Robin Muller;
illustrated by Suzanne Duranceau.
p.   cm.
Summary: At a special party hosted by an elegant cat,
the guests go in search of a beautiful hidden clock.
Based on the traditional nursery rhyme.
ISBN 0-590-47278-X
[1. Animals—Fiction. 2. Parties—Fiction.
3. Clocks and watches—Fiction. 4. Stores in rhyme.]
I. Duranceau, Suzanne, ill. II. Title.
PZ8.3.M874Hi   1993
[Fic]—DC20   92-37588
CIP
AC
12 11 10 9 8 7 6 5 4 3 2 1   3 4 5 6 7 8/9

Printed in the U.S.A.   37

First Scholastic printing, February 1994

To Lauren and Adam Traversy.
And to their brother Michael, who came just in time.
RM

To Alma and Sébastien.
And to my friends and assistants,
Tom Kapas and Luc Melanson,
with special thanks for their valuable contributions.
SD

Hickory, dickory, dock,
The cat has hidden the clock.
The clock struck one,
The hunt's begun.
Hickory, dickory, dock.

Gigglety, figglety, fare,
The goat looked under the chair.
The clock struck two,
The mouse yelled, "Boo!"
Gigglety, figglety, fare.

Margery, bargery, bow,
The monkey stubbed his toe.
The clock struck three,
He spilled the tea.
Margery, bargery, bow.

Tottery, pottery, pum,
The goat fell over the drum.
The clock struck four,
The mouse laughed, "More!"
Tottery, pottery, pum.

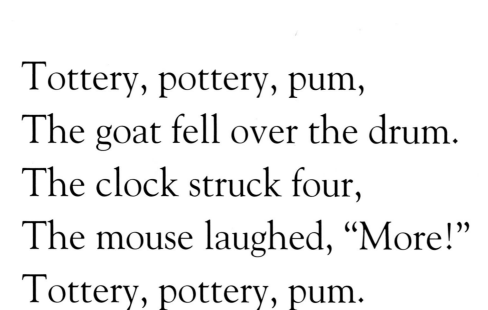

Hunkery, dunkery, day,
The lamb slid in on the tray.
The clock struck five,
The wolf arrived.
Hunkery, dunkery, day.

Tumberly, bumberly, boo,
The wolf fell into the glue.
The clock struck six,
He cried, "It sticks!"
Tumberly, bumberly, boo.

Ziggity, tiggity, tore,
The cow went through the floor.
The clock struck seven,
She fell from heaven.
Ziggity, tiggity, tore.

Higglety, pigglety, pot,
The goat untangled the knot.
The clock struck eight,
The cat cried, "Wait!"
Higglety, pigglety, pot.

11

Cattery, battery, bash,
The clock came down with a crash.
The clock struck nine,
"The fault is mine."
Cattery, battery, bash.

Rackety, knackety, knob,
They all began to sob.
The clock clunked ten,
"I'll fix it again!"
Rackety, knackety, knob,

Fiddlety, biddlety, bime,
The mouse repaired the time.
The clock struck eleven,
And all was forgiven.
Fiddlety, biddlety, bime.

Hickory, dickory, date,
"It's time to celebrate!"
The midnight hour
Has magic power . . .

Hickory, dickory, date.